Dear Parent:
Your child's love of reading starts here!

Every child learns to read in a different way and at his or her own speed. Some go back and forth between reading levels and read favorite books again and again. Others read through each level in order. You can help your young reader improve and become more confident by encouraging his or her own interests and abilities. From books your child reads with you to the first books he or she reads alone, there are I Can Read Books for every stage of reading:

SHARED READING
Basic language, word repetition, and whimsical illustrations, ideal for sharing with your emergent reader

BEGINNING READING
Short sentences, familiar words, and simple concepts for children eager to read on their own

READING WITH HELP
Engaging stories, longer sentences, and language play for developing readers

READING ALONE
Complex plots, challenging vocabulary, and high-interest topics for the independent reader

ADVANCED READING
Short paragraphs, chapters, and exciting themes for the perfect bridge to chapter books

I Can Read Books have introduced children to the joy of reading since 1957. Featuring award-winning authors and illustrators and a fabulous cast of beloved characters, I Can Read Books set the standard for beginning readers.

A lifetime of discovery begins with the magical words **"I Can Read!"**

Visit www.icanread.com for information
on enriching your child's reading experience.

For Anne and Antonio—
keep soaring above the weather!—H. P.

For Chloe, Scott, Ellie, and Ben, the chair,
the stuffed animals, the poses, your love . . .
and for Chloe getting out from
under the weather!—L. A.

The full-color cover artwork was created with gouache paint on paper, and the interior artwork was created on a Wacom Cintiq screen using Adobe PhotoShop.

I Can Read Book is a trademark of HarperCollins Publishers. Amelia Bedelia is a registered trademark of Peppermint Partners, LLC. Amelia Bedelia Under the Weather. Text copyright © 2019 by Herman S. Parish III. Illustrations copyright © 2019 by Lynne Avril. All rights reserved. No part of this book may be used or reproduced in any manner whatsoever without written permission except in the case of brief quotations embodied in critical articles and reviews. Manufactured in U.S.A. For information address HarperCollins Children's Books, a division of HarperCollins Publishers, 195 Broadway, New York, NY 10007.
www.icanread.com

Library of Congress Control Number: 2018949826

ISBN 978-0-06-265892-0 (hardback)—ISBN 978-0-06-265891-3 (pbk. ed.)

18 19 20 21 22 LSCC 10 9 8 7 6 5 4 3 2   First Edition

Greenwillow Books

I Can Read!

BEGINNING
1
READING

Amelia Bedelia
·Under the Weather·

by **Herman Parish** ❀ pictures by **Lynne Avril**

🏛 Greenwillow Books, *An Imprint of HarperCollinsPublishers*

Amelia Bedelia did not feel well.

She snuggled down in bed

with her stuffed animals.

"ROAR! What a zoo!"

said Amelia Bedelia's father.

"ACHOO!" said Amelia Bedelia.

"Do not tease her, honey.

She does not feel well,"

said Amelia Bedelia's mother.

Amelia Bedelia coughed.

"I am sorry that you are

under the weather,"

said Amelia Bedelia's father.

"I am not," said Amelia Bedelia.

"I am under my covers."

Amelia Bedelia felt dizzy.

She fell back on her pillow.

"You are sick," said her mother.

"I am calling the school.

You are staying home today."

Amelia Bedelia was happy.

Then she was sad.

"I will miss my friends," she said.

"I do not want to rain on your parade,"
said her mother,
"but something is going around."
"Not me," said Amelia Bedelia.
"I am staying here."

Before he left for work,
Amelia Bedelia's father
carried her
downstairs.

He tucked her in
to his special chair.
"Thanks, Daddy,"
said Amelia Bedelia.
"I will check on you
later," he said.

12

"You may have a fever,"
said Amelia Bedelia's mother.
"I will find a thermometer
to take your temperature."
She turned on the TV.

"Not the weather," said Amelia Bedelia.

"The weather is boring."

She did not have the energy to

change the channel.

She sighed.

"I am under the weather," she said.

"And now I am in front of it, too."

Amelia Bedelia did not know
why grown-ups worried
about the weather.

Whether it would rain.

Whether
it would snow.

Whether it would freeze

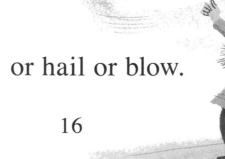

or hail or blow.

16

Amelia Bedelia never worried about it.

She had fun in all kinds of weather.

17

Amelia Bedelia's mother

put a thermometer

under Amelia Bedelia's tongue.

"I will be right back," her mother said.

THE WORLD

Amelia Bedelia watched the weather

all over the world.

"Ey ook! Eets wane hats een hogs!"
said Amelia Bedelia.

Her mother took the thermometer
out of Amelia Bedelia's mouth.
"What did you say?" she asked.

"Hey, look!

It is raining cats and dogs!"

said Amelia Bedelia.

"Poor sweetie," said her mother.

"You have a little fever."

The telephone rang.

It was Amelia Bedelia's father.

"Hey, sunshine," he said.

"How are you?"

"I am sick," said Amelia Bedelia.

"Are you feeling

green around the gills?"

her father asked.

Just then there was a knock
at the door.

"Yoo-hoo! Howdy, neighbor,"
said Mrs. Adams.

"It is raining buckets out there!"

"And cats and dogs, too,"
said Amelia Bedelia.

YOO-HOO!

"I hear you are not feeling so hot,"
said Mrs. Adams.

"I am feeling very hot,"
said Amelia Bedelia.

"Amelia Bedelia is running a fever,"
said her mother.

"I am way too sick to run,"
said Amelia Bedelia.

"Well, I have something good
for what is making you sick,"
said Mrs. Adams. "Chicken soup!"

"Thank you," said Amelia Bedelia.
"But I need something bad
for what is making me sick."

"Do you have a stomach bug?"
asked Mrs. Adams.

"Yuck!" said Amelia Bedelia.

"I hope not!"

YUCK!!

"You have some kind of bug, sweetie,"
said Amelia Bedelia's mother.
"I wish it had wings,"
said Amelia Bedelia.
"Then I could fly above the weather,
instead of being under it."

Amelia Bedelia's father came home.

The weather was still on TV.

"You must be on top of the weather,"

he said.

"It will be partly

cloudy tomorrow,"

said Amelia Bedelia.

"Not partly sunny?"
asked her father.

"Daddy, that is the same thing!"
said Amelia Bedelia.

31

"You must be feeling better,"
said Amelia Bedelia's father.
"Soon you will be as right as rain,"
said her mother.
"Come rain or shine!"
said Amelia Bedelia.